WHO?

Written and Illustrated by Joan Hutson

St. Paul Books & Media

WHO SAYS, "NIGHT IS DONE" TO THE MORNING SUN?

WHO SAYS, "NO MORE SITTIN'" TO THE LAZY KITTEN?

WHO SAYS, "CATERPILLAR, CRAWL, YOU WON'T FALL!"?

WHO SAYS, "CRICKET, SING, IT'S SPRING!"?

WHO SAYS, "YOU CAN'T!" TO THE ANT?

WHO SAYS, "SING A TUNE" TO THE NEWBORN LOON?

WHO
SAYS,
"BECOME
A RAM,
LITTLE LAMB"?

12

WHO SAYS, "RACE THROUGH THE AIR, LITTLE MARE?"

WHO SAYS, "MAKE A WISH, LITTLE STAR FISH"?

16

WHO SAYS, "EAGLE, SOAR, MORE, ...MORE, ... MORE ..."

WHO SAYS, "FLY HIGH THROUGH THE SKY" TO THE EAGER DUCK?

20

WHO SAYS, "HUSH"
TO THE
THUNDER'S
CRUSH?

21

WHO SAYS, "YOU ARE FREED, AUTUMN SEED"?

WHO SAYS,
"SNOWFLAKE,
DANCE HIGH
THROUGH THE SKY"?

WHO SAYS, "SNUGGLE THERE, SNOWSHOE HARE"?

WHO SAYS, "LITTLE PINE, YOU COULD BE A CHRISTMAS TREE"?

WHO SAYS, "I KNOW EVERY REASON WHY CHILDREN CRY..."?

AND EVERY REASON WHY CHILDREN SMILE...

WHO SAYS,

"I LOVE

YOU"?

I KNOW WHO!

28

AND

I DO

TOO!

St. Paul Book & Media Centers

ALASKA
750 West 5th Ave., Anchorage, AK 99501 907-272-8183.
CALIFORNIA
3908 Sepulveda Blvd., Culver City, CA 90230 310-397-8676.
1570 Fifth Ave. (at Cedar Street), San Diego, CA 92101 619-232-1442; 619-232-1443.
46 Geary Street, San Francisco, CA 94108 415-781-5180.
FLORIDA
145 S.W. 107th Ave., Miami, FL 33174 305-559-6715; 305-559-6716.
HAWAII
1143 Bishop Street, Honolulu, HI 96813 808-521-2731.
ILLINOIS
172 North Michigan Ave., Chicago, IL 60601 312-346-4228; 312-346-3240.
LOUISIANA
4403 Veterans Memorial Blvd., Metairie, LA 70006 504-887-7631; 504-887-0113.
MASSACHUSETTS
50 St. Paul's Ave., Jamaica Plain, Boston, MA 02130 617-522-8911.
Rte. 1, 885 Providence Hwy., Dedham, MA 02026 617-326-5385.
MISSOURI
9804 Watson Rd., St. Louis, MO 63126 314-965-3512; 314-965-3571.

NEW JERSEY
561 U.S. Route 1, Wick Plaza, Edison, NJ 08817 908-572-1200.
NEW YORK
150 East 52nd Street, New York, NY 10022 212-754-1110.
78 Fort Place, Staten Island, NY 10301 718-447-5071; 718-447-5086.
OHIO
2105 Ontario Street (at Prospect Ave.), Cleveland, OH 44115 216-621-9427.
PENNSYLVANIA
214 W. DeKalb Pike, King of Prussia, PA 19406 215-337-1882; 215-337-2077.
SOUTH CAROLINA
243 King Street, Charleston, SC 29401 803-577-0175.
TEXAS
114 Main Plaza, San Antonio, TX 78205 512-224-8101.
VIRGINIA
1025 King Street, Alexandria, VA 22314 703-549-3806.
CANADA
3022 Dufferin Street, Toronto, Ontario, Canada M6B 3T5 416-781-9131.

Hutson, Joan.
　　Who? / written and illustrated by Joan Hutson.
　　　　p.　　cm.
　　ISBN 0-8198-8266-6
　　1. God—Juvenile literature. I. Title.
BT107.H88 1992
231—dc20
　　　　　　　　　　　　　　　　92-31811
　　　　　　　　　　　　　　　　CIP

Printed and published in the U.S.A. by St. Paul Books & Media, 50 St. Paul's Avenue, Boston, MA 02130
St. Paul Books & Media is the publishing house of the Daughters of St. Paul, an international congregation of women religious serving the Church with the communications media.

1 2 3 4 5 6 7 8 9 　　　　　　　　　　　　　　　99 98 97 96 95 94 93 92